RECUPERA

by EMMA GOMIS

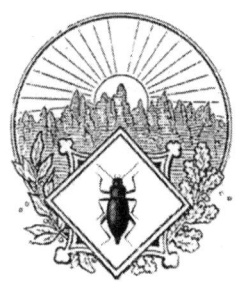

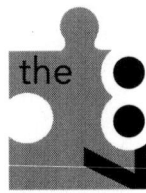

Published 2025 by the87press

The 87 Press LTD

87 Stonecot Hill

Sutton

Surrey

SM3 9HJ

www.the87press.co.uk

ISBN: 9781068644689

Printed and bound by Aquatint, Units 3-4 Elm Grove Ind Estate, Elm Grove, Wimbledon SW19 4HE

Design: Stanislava Stoilova [www.sdesign.graphics]

To my sister
(in correspondence & complicity)

Feta desig, cant i paraula
et miro. Jo sóc tu mateixa.
No em reconec: sóc l'altra.

—Maria Mercè Marçal

Made desire, song and word
I look at you. I am you.
I don't recognize myself: I am the other.

—Maria Mercè Marçal (author's translation)

Confessional writing is always self-performative. To call this book nonfiction isn't totally true but calling it fiction would belie its sincerity. It is something in between. As with all tellings, mine are skewed and slanted. They are personal and impersonal. They don't adhere to a straight chronology. They meander. The theoretical and literary texts quoted throughout are texts that were keeping company with my thinking and so have made their way into the writing. They are lifted and recontextualized because my attention turned towards them.

CONTENTS

Memory is a Ghost

I can't remember if it was day or night when we left. We hauled all of our possessions out of the house, down the narrow stairway, and on to the street. You were so angry you weren't speaking to me, but we were moving together in tacit understanding.

What I always remember, were the days leading up to our departure. The series of dramatic moments unfolding into each other, carrying forward a hysterical impulse, portending an inevitable end. I remember the night before spent opening every zipper of my purse, checking every pocket, digging my fingers into the fabric. Our parents crying.

It was winter when we left for Recupera. The internet flickered. Our teeth chattered. I remember the ice coating the surfaces of the city more than I remember being cold.

I.

MY CATALOGUE OF CASTS

What are the limits of the body?
—Akilah Oliver[1]

Dear Sister,

Since Recupera life in Colorado has felt slow. I feel like I am in a nineteenth century novel, out in the countryside, 'getting well,' but a more rustic Wild West version. The wind rips through the canyon and shakes the cabin. The woods, their space and hollow, offer me a clearance to get myself together and write.

I've filled notebook after notebook. One of them is the one you gave me for my birthday the first summer I spent here. On the cover, a collaged grid of squares, each with a different photo of yourself — alternate versions of yourself. In one of them, your hair is red, in another black, in another blonde. In one of them, your face is caked in makeup, in another you wear none. Towards the middle of the cover, you typed out in a gothic font: 'Sister Emma's Questions and Concerns'. After you left, I kept it on my desk and when a question surfaced, I wrote it down. The questions piled, multiplying only into more questions and no answers. List after list after list. I formed a habit. My lists littered the surface of my desk, my kitchen table. Overwhelmed, I searched for threads to consolidate my research. You always like a good pop quiz, so I thought I could send you some of my questions. In this first one my enquiry constellated around the body.

List 1.

> How much can a body endure, and when does it
> fold in exhaustion upon itself?
> Where do we carry each other?
> What inheritance marks our shape?
> What constrictions limit our movements?

What kind of information is stored?
What causes the body to break down?

I think of you every day and miss you very much.

Love,
E

~

When you come to visit, I pick you up in my rusted red 1991 Isuzu Trooper, *The Cure* blasting through the speakers. On the drive home you tell me you feel like you've trashed your body. You keep getting sick. The rumination has subsided but now they've found cysts; they aren't cancerous, but they also weren't there before. 'Monday you can fall apart, Tuesday, Wednesday break my heart...' Your moment of vulnerability catches me off guard and I look out the window. I feel that dropping sensation into my gut. I should have said something comforting, maybe told you that mine is trashed too. That hearing about your pain paralyses me with a want to take it from you. That I also carry expressions of the same hurt. We poisoned our bodies and they broke down — not in neat pieces but in arrest and convulsion. I never again want to feel the shiver of withdrawal; the imprint of memory a deterrent enough — my arms clasped around my body, doubled over.

~

You are now back in London and the distance imposes itself. Here in Colorado, as the snow starts to dust the trees, I've been trying to help you draft an artist statement for some grant you're applying to. I'm going over details, and here is what I remember:

Your career as a makeup artist started with a desire to shock people. You wanted to make gory objects, monstered creations and got that job in a studio in Los Angeles producing wounds and prosthetics. I remember the day you met me on Melrose Avenue with a fake gash bleeding on your arm, the skin ripped around the edges. You wore the wound around all afternoon. As we crossed the street, a tourist couple pulled their child towards them and said, 'this happens because they don't have free healthcare in the United States.' We walked into stores and people moved away, in one they asked you to leave. We sat at a restaurant and everyone around us averted their gaze. I can't remember much more of the day but what stayed with me was the image of the bloody prosthetic fixed to your arm, how every time I looked at it, I wanted to scream and help you, to cover the open wound with a bandage, how I wished it was on my arm instead.

~

Really, your artistic process and interest in prosthesis began much earlier as a childhood hobby. You used to make casts, cover your body in plaster to build artificial limbs, form moulds to practice the making of wounds. As we aged, you left pieces of yourself scattered around our various childhood homes. Different parts of your body in every nook and cranny — your ear, teeth, lips, hand. I expected a limb to protrude each time I opened a drawer. Made throughout your life, they weren't part of a cohesive project but just something that you did. You gave them away as gifts, mostly to me. Carrying pieces of you with me each time I move to a new place, they've since adorned every room I've lived in. As part of my ritual of unpacking, I unwrap your lips and place them on the bookshelf.

~

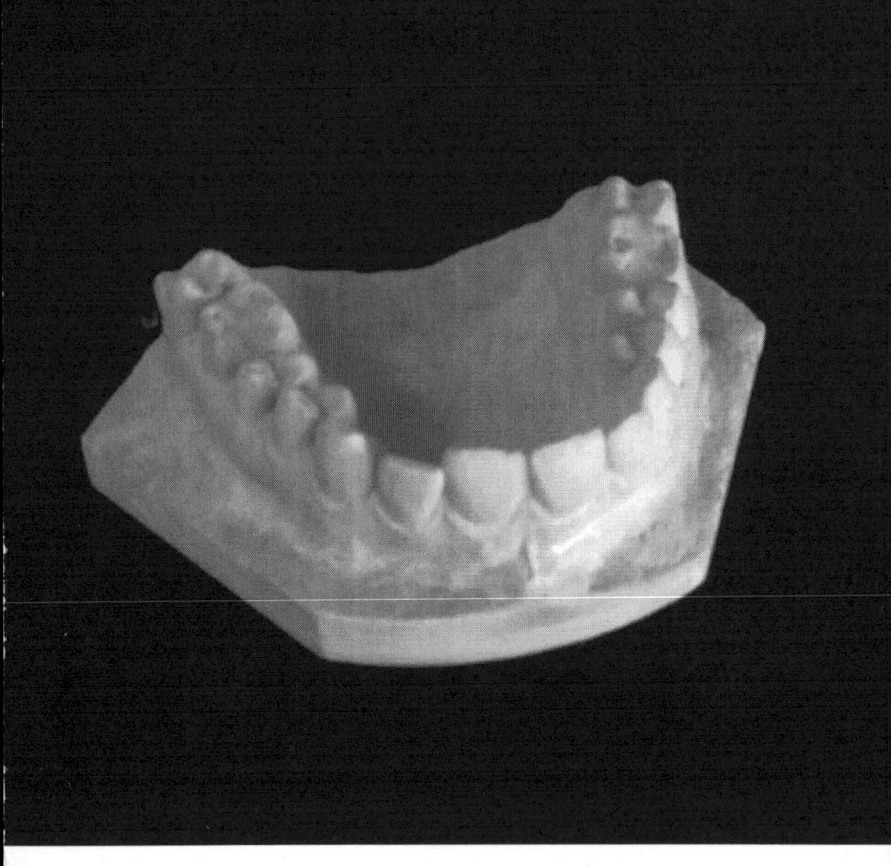

Teeth, 2006
Dental plaster, 2x3"

In the first months of living here, I barely left the cabin. I would descend from the mountains in order to buy food, attend the occasional lecture, meet with a childhood friend; but mostly I was secluded, solitary. During the years I've spent in Colorado your fragmented body has kept me company, Sister. The pieces are silent, as if in their severance the life had drained out, the lack of colour in the plaster a further disavowal of life. But despite their lack of animation, they have witnessed my writing, my process, my living.

Your bottom teeth I keep in the junk drawer of my bedside table. You were sixteen when the cast was made. Now, your teeth have eroded. Ground to stumps in your sleep, you've encased them in gold. Covered the chips with shine, coated over the decay. I know you love the way grills look but I was surprised when you decided to get diamonds and jewels glued onto your canines. Your fascination with cosmetic adjustments continually evolving, the casts capturing moments of a body in constant transformation, serving as a technology of memory. Recording fragments of time, each cast recalls your body in a specific temporality, serving as a tangible object, a memory aid, a record, a ghost. The casts become altered reproductions of the current manifestation, shifting between negative and positive, you enact a process of documentation, creating a corporeal archive. I've become its custodian.

~

Our grandmother's teeth are rotting out; our mother uses whitening strips. I ask our grandmother to take out her dentures and place them in a glass for a photo; I ask our mother if I can try one of her whitening strips. Brushing across enamel and gum we engage in a barely audible, private, yet communal ritual.

~

Dear Sister,

Here is List #2, another pop quiz.

> When we brush our teeth in different countries, do
> our gestures align?
> Is our chewing synchronic? A twinned sweep. A
> mirror. A reflection that doubles as we see each
> other in ourselves?
> What index would we make if we could archive all
> the things we have bitten into?

Love,
E

~

I run my tongue over my teeth and feel the topography of my inner landscape. In a recurring dream my teeth fall out, crumble, shatter. I wake up and write it down. I place the mould of your teeth on top and use it as a paper weight. The mould is a cast of your body from the specific moment when a dentist pressed the silicone against the roof of your mouth and asked you to bite down, hold still. In those months of nightmares and panic — a lingering residue of our drug addiction, or part of the process of recovery — there was a sense of calm I found through repetition: the act of hypnagogic writing followed by placing your teeth on top of my words, as if the weight might keep them tethered.

~

The plaster chips in places. I move the teeth outside and lay them in the pine needles. I take twenty-something steps back and turn to find they blend in with the landscape, the white of animal bone.

~

The dentist places the silicone in an impression tray designed to fit over the dental arches. I imagine you waiting, trying to decide if the goop pressed against the roof of your mouth is a pleasurable or uncomfortable sensation, the material setting to become an elastic solid. In a few minutes, it creates an imprint, or impression body. The impression body, a hollowed out negative space of the real/positive body, can cover the real like a glove, but without it remains a hollow cavity.

Once the impression tray is removed and the material has solidified, the impression body is filled with another type of material, and the artefact that results from the process is again a positive body, a reproduction of the initial body. The negative body translates once again into a positive body. The new positive body a nearly perfect translation of the real body.

We are so complete in our difference that sometimes I think you possess every quality I lack; you hold all the positive of my negative attributes. Your feet are a half size bigger, your torso longer than mine. Marked with our own idiosyncrasies, we also share similar features. Sometimes when I look at you, I see myself. In your movements I see my own, in your voice I hear mine. I start to wonder what kind of impressions we make upon each other.

~

List 3.

How can bodies translate or make impressions onto other bodies?
Are we negative and positive impressions of each other, Sister?
In the uncanny doubling of our gestures, in the matching tattoos we have of the sphinx lady with a snake tail, are we creating reproductions of each other, Sister?

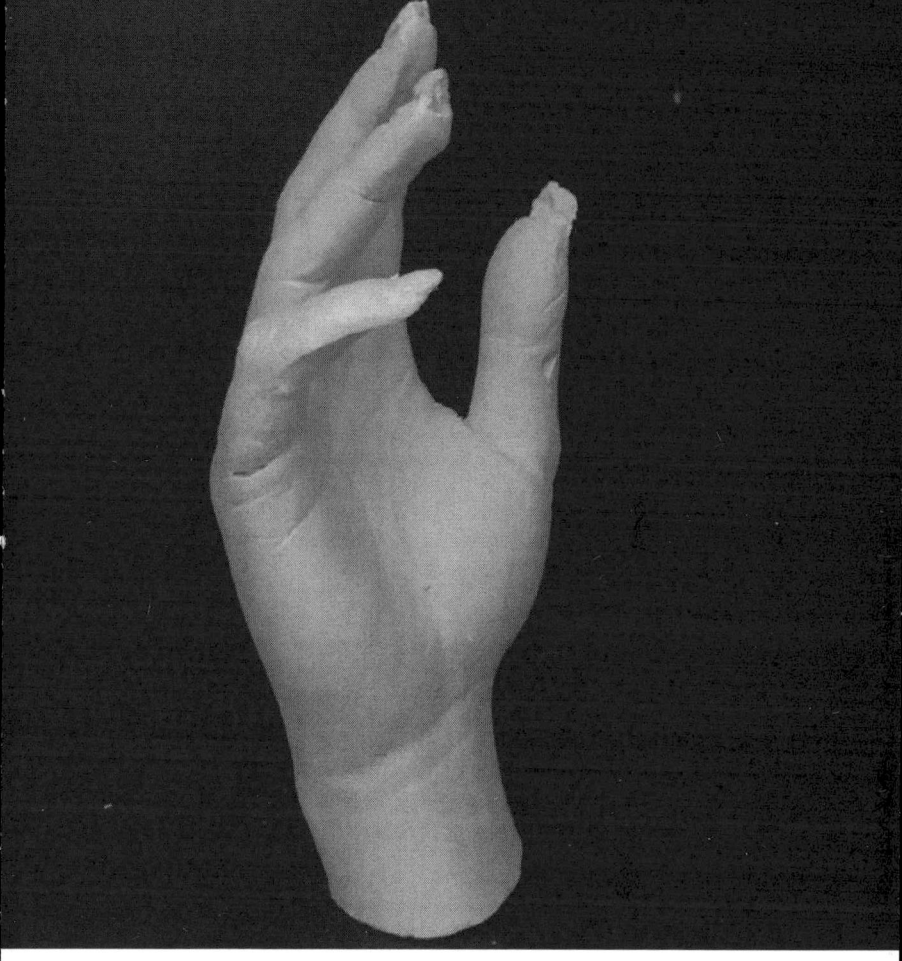

Hand, 2011
Plaster, 5x4"

My ritual of writing includes taking breaks to pace around the living room, staring at nothing, steeped in thought. On the mantel above the fireplace your doubled hand beckons, and I brush against the tips of your fingers absentmindedly, placing mine gently against yours.

The cast of your hand always makes me want to cry, the contour of the vein so familiar, the width of the fingers and shape of their form evocative of your ardent candour. I envy your bluntness, the way you stand, the graceful assurance in everything you do. Even when we were strung out, you had a way of making it seem elegant. You were so heroin-chic. We never shot up, that would have been too much, a blatant acknowledgement of our secret habit, but we hid sheets of tin foil in our purses and back pockets. We lived half-awake, in a dream of mixed pleasure and dulled pain, an unbearable daze too affective to ignore and too embarrassing to accept.

~

The tips of your fingers are chipped; the fissures in the plaster, fossils of darker times — when they shook from withdrawal, turned black, turned blue. The white cast remains cracked; but objects can be repaired, stories shoulder the unforeseeable, and everyone loves a comeback kid. We unlearned the techniques to ingest our drugs and traded in our utensils.

Given a tool, the hand is transformed, morphs into different iterations of itself, becomes something generative, a process of renovation. In London, it held the tools to destroy the body, a rolled-up sheet of aluminium to catch the trail of smoke burning off a piece of brown, the gestures and rituals of addiction. Now yours hold tools to transform the face: a makeup brush, an eyeliner, providing the affordances to become someone else, a recasting, a performance of identity. You coat your eyelids with shadows and highlight the architecture of your bones.

Similarly, the pencil, or computer, has endowed my hands with an impression of my voice, and allows me to communicate with you despite the distance between us. The hand can endure, can mend and revamp itself. We engaged in a new process of becoming.

~

My process of becoming has involved a new relationship to order. A ritualisation of my life dispels the memories that were too painful to face. My lists and catalogues make me feel a sense of stability and progress. We've never spoken about what happened, our silence, a vow to move forward, or a refusal to acknowledge our shame.

Your cast hand fraternises with my hush. It silently remains severed both from your body and from time, becoming an event out of time, a pocket into the past. Despite the different modalities of transport and many journeys it's been on, it hasn't decomposed but remains intact, a relic. Your artefact-hand is fragile, but I transport it tenderly, supporting it with wads of tissue so it stands up in a shoebox, so that it doesn't bounce in the back of my truck and end up a pile of shards — half a finger, a piece of wrist.

~

Your natural hands are more resilient than the silent white plaster; they speak in loud gestures, they move with the rhythm of your improvisations, wringing with worry, your nails gnawed to the flesh. Laden with rings of gold and onyx, they move to punctuate your flow of thought. As I watch them move and choreograph your thinking, I consider a theory of punctuation based on the interrupting gestures of your body, an improvised movement with its own idiosyncratic motions and commas, a presocratic rhythm punctuating your conversational flow.

The thought is left behind, the lines remain as an impression, a record, a cast of my thinking, something to return to. Text is malleable; it morphs and transforms as we save and delete, command, undo; our external memory device fails us, the technologies of archiving falter. The draft is not a cast but an impression body.

The casts were never meant to be put on display but rather impulses you materialised and left scattered. One day, moved by the realisation that they had become an implicit part of my daily routine, I gathered them and took photographs, I started my catalogue.

~

Some days I pick your hand up off of the mantel and, holding it in my grip, move and gesticulate as if it were an extension of my own body. In these moments, I am reminded of the day we trodded across the concrete of the South Bank and made our way to the Tate Modern where we encountered the Austrian artist Franz West's 'Adaptables', those bizarre protrusions. The *Paßstücke* sculptures (translated as 'Fitting Pieces,' 'Adaptives' or 'Adaptables') West produced in the 1970s embody the same nonconformity and malleable shape of your fragmented form.

The sculptural objects had once been ordinary items, discarded and found, which West covered with coats of white plaster, allowing them to become something else entirely. There is something familiar about the objects, but they are also completely unrecognisable, blurry. In the gallery, we were encouraged to pick up the adaptables, to consider them as extensions of our own bodies, but the pieces were heavy and the movements awkward. We stood in front of a mirror trying to dance or play with the strange biomorphic shapes. Too heavy to pick up with one hand, I wielded mine like a sword, heaving it into the air, then letting the tip land on the floor and circling around it as if the choreography might smooth out the clunkiness of my movements. You cradled yours in the nook of your elbow while you sauntered up to the mirror, then held it out in front of you and swung it up and down as if trying to shake life into it.

What these adaptables offered us was a chance to experiment with our bodies, to take a strange indistinct object and incorporate it as if it were a part of our own physicality, to be playful, to accept the bizarre and allow room for a body that didn't support a hegemonic normality, but instead offered something else — a new perception of our physical realities.

~

I show a draft of this manuscript to a few friends, and they tell me that it feels like I am writing an elegy, even though you're not dead.

The first tattoo you ever got was a black and white detailed portrait of my face covering your entire forearm. I look back over my shoulder, my hair pinned around my face. A seemingly elegiac depiction of a loved one, people often ask how I passed. The tattoo evokes a lament. I wonder what it is that makes us treat each other this way. Why we insist on externalising one another, why we praise each other with a devotion usually reserved for the dead. Why each time I play a song on the piano you cry as if it were a dirge. Why you keep refusing to read this manuscript.

~

One Sunday, when the mist came in and rendered the mountains opaque, ghostly outlines; I asked X to take photographs of my body. We decided the shots would be up close, so I could use them later for a self-examination, an analysis; so I could print them out and place them next to your casts to examine our difference. He pointed the 4x5 camera towards the bed. We started with my neutral hand. I was an object positioned and observed. When he tucked my hair behind my ear, I felt beautiful. When I held a magnifying glass in front of my mouth to get a close up of my teeth, I posed, defiant. Then he asked to photograph my nipple crossed by an afternoon shaft of light. He touched it to make it hard. I was sexed. When he asked me to lay on my back and spread my legs, I felt exposed. I was uncomfortable but posed as he asked me to. This was your idea, he said.

When things are exposed, they can then be analysed. To reveal something allows us to interpret it. Analysis requires a taking apart and putting back together. I try to analyse our likeness, our difference. Where are we the same, identical? Where do we split off, diverge? Would you have said stop or said no?

The photograph of my ear comes out blurry. In the image, it is hard to discern what the curved shape resembles, like a strange protrusion sticking out from an indistinct bulge of grey.

~

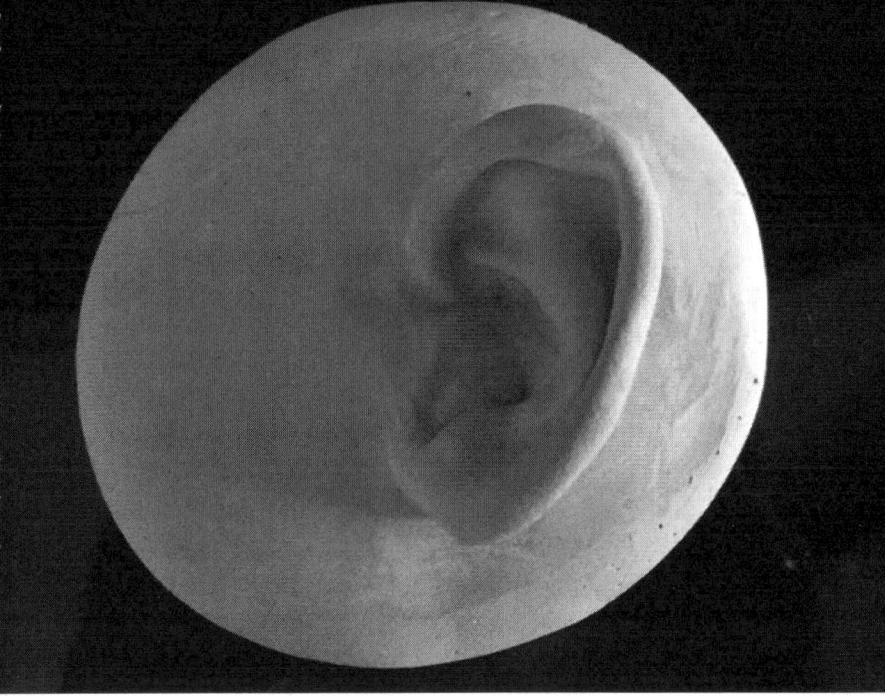

Ear, 2016
Plaster 3 x 4"

In Colorado, time moves at strange speeds. Sometimes, I write for hours, sometimes for minutes, both increments feel equal, approximate. I enter atemporal lacunae, get lost in thought staring into the pines, watching a carbon black crow loiter on the bannister.

Sister, your ear sits on my coffee table, eternalised. Sometimes, I pick it up by the lobe and move it onto another stack of books where it rings patiently. It folds and curves upon itself, encouraging a making of words. A covert organ of balance, the canal here is blocked by cement. Your left ear, usually ornamented with gold hoops of different sizes, punctured along the rim, lays bare and grey.

When you came to visit, we talked about reproducing it, along with other cast appendages, placing and arranging them in the woods to create an optical illusion — a graveyard of body parts decomposing into the earth, hidden by leaves, grown over with lichen and moss.

~

For years you made drawings of the ear mouse you wanted to get tattooed on your back, your fascination with the grotesque ever-present. I thought it was a fictional monster you had fabricated until you made me look it up — the laboratory Vacanti Mouse with an ear-shaped protrusion of cartilage sticking out of its back. The images made me feel sick, but I couldn't turn away. Clicking through articles, I found out more: the surgeons and brothers Joseph and Charles Vacanti were primarily responsible for initiating the field of tissue engineering in medicine. Experimenting with methods that could allow them to generate human body parts, their research worked towards addressing organ shortage. They implanted an ear-shaped piece of cartilage, formed by seeding cow cartilage cells, under the skin of the mouse.

~

List 4.

What is the future of the prosthetic limb, of the body? Did the addition of an ear-shaped cartilage to the body of the mouse, represent the possible dangers of body alteration as well as potential progress in the medical field?

How are good and bad contained within the same capacious metaphor?

As bodies are altered, does their original shape soften? Do we obscure by adding and become vague?

~

It was snowing one day, and I texted to see how you were doing. I was feeling cold and numb. We exchanged notes about the weather and about distance, then you wrote:

> Also interesting fact…your clitoris will grow throughout your life….your birthday is coming!
> Wow, that is interesting.
> The biggest one is reportedly 12 inches long. Earlobes also keep growing.

> 12 inches? How is that possible?

I put down my phone and opened a book. I flipped randomly and, by the strange assertions of bibliomancy, the book landed on Hans Bellmer's doll photographs. Composites of different body parts mashed together to form grotesquely beautiful hybrid bodies. The dolls are distorted. My eyes glued to the page, somewhat repulsed but engrossed as I scanned over the bulging and fused fleshy forms.

~

When you were a kid, you took a Barbie doll and sliced off her breasts, cut off all of her hair and dyed the spiky remains dark blue. I always thought that had you been given more than one doll you would have assembled hybrid creatures, forming strange composite bodies. When I ask you about it, you tell me that you just didn't have a Ken doll and felt embarrassed to ask our parents for a man so Barbie would have someone to make out with. Despite our grandfather being openly gay, society had still conditioned us with heteronormative assumptions.

After you had your trans Barbie make out with your cis Barbie, you threw the trans Barbie onto the roof, hoping no one would ever know. A few weeks later, our dad found him while cleaning out the gutters. I remember thinking it was so strange and wonderful, the blue hair, the total transformation of the doll I had seen the day before.

~

X always called me an exhibitionist because I like to walk around nude. When we lived in Barcelona, the humidity and heat made me want to stand naked on the balcony to feel the breeze running past the linen curtains. A family from Morocco lived across the street with five little boys. After catching a glimpse of my naked body leaning over the bannister, they started ringing the doorbell of our apartment building, then giggling and running away. X told me I should cover my body. We lived on one of the narrowest streets in the whole of the city, and it was inevitable that someone would see me naked. I said it was probably the most fun those boys had, and I didn't want to take that away from them. To be honest, I just didn't want him telling me what to do with my body. I liked the idea that the kids were around the corner gossiping about the naked woman on the balcony. As if I had become a myth, some neighbourhood folklore.

Hans Bellmer wrote that 'all dreams return again to the only remaining instinct, to escape from the outline of the self'.[2] Is that what I was trying to do by becoming a myth? Is that what you were trying to do in making the plaster casts? What is it that links exhibitionism to shame? The space we traverse between, a paradox we straddle to cover up one with the other. What would a composite outline look like? One that is not of the self but of the many selves?

~

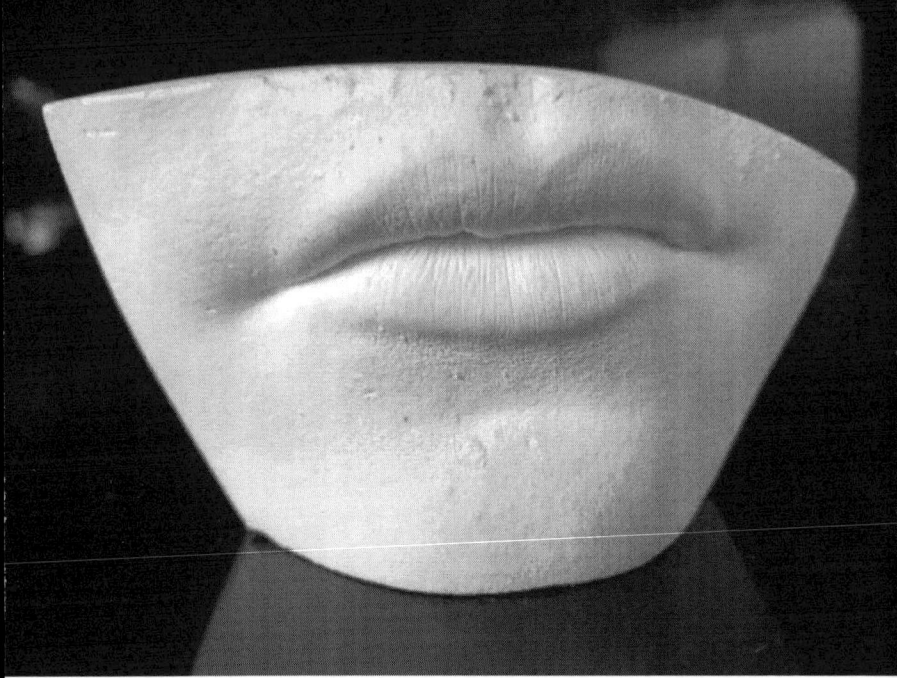

Lips, 2009
Plaster 3 x 3 "

We are both always one and always many; we are similar and also split.

Sometimes we finish each other's sentences, sometimes we speak together when we speak to each other. Sometimes we don't speak for weeks, maybe a month, but you always inform the words I make. They are pliant, they bend and move and roll around in my mouth, over my soft tongue, my throat opens before they leave my lips.

Your lips you paint purple, orange, rouge. You outline, contour, and apply thick colours as if they were a convex canvas.

The cast of your lips is so exact that I almost wait for them to open. But they sit on my bookshelf and remain pressed. Sometimes I imagine what they would say if they parted, how they would engage in a dialogue with the texts they live among. The anticipation of your voice is so near I can almost hear it.

~

Our lips are an intimate part of the body. An erogenous zone that we also use as a vehicle for expression. When you send me letters, they come with a red kiss on the crease where the envelope is lick-sealed.

Our lips part open and things enter and exit our bodies. They wrapped around our tools as we ingested our drugs. Sometimes I think my body wanted to die but was so numb it couldn't discern between a death wish and hedonism. Or maybe it didn't want to die but it *was* dying and trying to tell me, I just wouldn't listen. I have spent so much time wondering what happened, what was broken and led to those harrowing limits. Under those conditions of unfeeling, there was no listening to my body except to feed it with more drugs when it cried out in shivers, then suffer the side effects of what kept it alive. I felt nauseous and sick all of the time. Did you feel the same? We never talked about it; just put on music and swayed around our rooms while our skin greyed. Ultimately, I've come to perceive it as the cliché of a train wreck in slow motion, one that tore us open like one of your wounds.

~

I am constantly mourning little deaths. With each transformation your body has gone through, I miss the previous incarnation. With each new tattoo you get, I mourn your innocent skin. With each gory wound you fabricate, I grieve an imaginary flesh. Each time you apply your makeup I wish your bare face would come through. The lament lives with me. The casts I arrange in my house memorialising your younger selves, little altars to your transformations and my own.

~

Pop Quiz

E: How much can a body endure, and when does it fold in exhaustion upon itself?

A: Nothing or everything. It folds sometimes the second you're awake.

E: Where do we carry each other?

A: Everywhere. Good and terrible places. Piggy all the way. Piggyback.

E: What inheritance marks our shape?

A: A concoction of soldiers, hippies, artists, two-thumbed-drunks, unemployed bohos, international schools, lost freaks. Our shape is 4ever changing. We come from nowhere, shape shifters, true blood. We never hit the mark.

E: What constrictions limit our movements?

A: Jeans and bras, money, exhaustion, making decisions.

E: What kind of information is stored inside of us?

A: Bullshit tips and tricks.

E: What causes the body to break down?

A: Absolutely everything.

Notes from Recupera

March 6ᵗʰ, 2016

If memory is a seamstress, our garments have been similarly stitched. You often say, 'we are cut from the same cloth'. Ariadne used to dress us in matching clothes and sew our name tags into the collars, but how closely did our threads align? Our Avia taught us how to weave Catalan Lace, the gentle clicking of the wooden bobbins being tossed between our hands in sync across the pillow, our movements mirroring each other with the swiftness of the *puntaires* as we wove the delicate textile.

We arrived in Recupera three days ago and since being here I can only seem to think about our childhood, our first years in Catalunya. I will keep a record in this notebook. You are still sleeping, so for now I will write you a letter:

Dear Sister,

Do you look to the same objects to recall the trace of an experience? Does the sound of the wooden bobbins evoke in you the same calm it does me? Is our family mythology composed of the same scenes, the same acts, the same gestures?

Love,
E

~

Some of my most vivid aesthetic memories are of playing with black beetles at our family farmhouse in the *Montnegre*, the black mountain of Catalunya. Catching them in buckets, watching them disappear through cracks in the wall, under rocks. How they would move so slowly across the ground, or over our hands as we brought them up to our eyes to inspect them closely. The funny sour smell when we found one dead in the toilet or mashed into the terracotta floor of the patio by a careless footstep.

On that black mountain, I wrote down the details of our games, while you finger painted next to me. Your imagination always blooming and wild, mine — a driven necessity to document.

Persuading our cousins to stand in as actors, we wrote anti-monarchic plays we put on in the fields behind the farmhouse; the cops spoke in Spanish, the civilians in Catalan. We would dress up in whatever we could fashion, old sheets, and discarded sun hats and, with our parents, aunts, uncles, and Avia sitting as audience, the production would unfold. Beetles inching across the stage.

~

March 8ᵗʰ, 2016

My recovery has involved a return to this shared history, a mining through the details of our childhood, longing for more innocent experience. In Recupera, time moves at strange speeds — slow, slower, slower-yet. Things emerge and intrude upon the day. The bright, blinding light shining on every corner. The memories that surface seem to linger. When I sit staring out at the water, they appear as scenes and acts. At times I feel as if I'm scripting one of our childhood plays.

~

March 8ᵗʰ, 2016

[ACT I / Scene i / location: the black mountain / afternoon]

The whole family, some 20-something people, sits out on the patio of the farmhouse.

All (sing): Escarabat Bum Bum. Posa'hi oli posa'hi oli. Escarbat Bum Bum. Posa'hi oli en el llum.

The lyrics of the song translate to scarab boom boom, put oil in the lamp. They are all patting you on the back while singing the refrain followed by *little scarab, guess who hit you?* Then uncle Sevi taps you and you whip around to guess who it was. If you guess wrong, the singing and tapping starts up again.

~

March 8th, 2016

[ACT I / Scene ii / location: the black mountain / evening]

Uncle Sevi leads a few of the children around the back of the house. Over the course of his life, he has amassed a collection of plastic bags which he keeps in boxes in the shed, the wooden doors clamped together by broken locks. He opens a box, ripping duct tape from the seams, and pulls the bags out carefully, one by one, as if examining an archive of capitalism. I remember your face — eyes wide in fascination.

~

II.

THE BIRTHDAY PARTY

Close proximities, frictions, melding. When I acknowledge my body is intimately connected to your body (we affect each other), we can no longer categorize individual disabilities. Bodies are about and between *bodies.*

—*Brenda Iijima*[3]

To write about film is to write about history, and to write about history is to choose which histories to tell. That's what I thought after reading the email you sent me late last night:

From: My Sister
Subject: no rushhhhh all chill vibes
Date: December 12, 2018 at 12:33:33 AM GMT
To: Emma Gomis

Dear sister Emma,

I hope this finds you well.
Have you watched any good movies lately?
I love you more than you'll ever know. Oh god I might cryyy nooo new moon vibes! We got this.

Many thanks,

Andrea Rose

I started drafting an email back knowing it would be too long and you would never likely read it but welcoming the impulse nonetheless. I wanted to write in the tempo of the visual frame, the topic moved me towards trying to claim an impossible horizon. I wanted to write about every film at once. My indecision plagued me, followed me like an unwelcome ghost as I paced the room reminded that the word dilemma has my name embedded within it. But there was one film that kept recurring in my hauntings. So finally, I decided, I would write to you about Sally Potter and her film *The Party*.

~

Sally Potter's film has a simple premise: a group of friends are invited to a dinner party in London to celebrate Janet's promotion to the political position of Shadow Health Minister. As the evening unfolds, a series of revealing confrontations and dialogue expose betrayal and hypocrisy. It's a witty commentary on bourgeois self-involvement that was shot over the fortnight during which the Brexit referendum took place. That same fortnight, as the world seemed to unspool violently, so did our lives; we were in London, each unable to help the other, with time warping unsteady beneath us. A few days later we were on our way to Recupera, the politics of the world mirroring our personal despair. Our friends fell away like the ground slowly receding in the aeroplane window. Potter's film does what I have still been unable to do — it turns to satire as a way of addressing tragedy.

~

Dear A,

In your email you put the noun *sister* before my name, as if I were a nun in a monastery or fighting in a revolution. I write to you as if you are me, as if we are the same. It is you that falls and scrapes your knee, but I bear your scar. I fell into the pond where the turtle bit your hand. In our sistering we rebel against categorization, and *rebel* and *revel* have the same roots.

Love,
E

~

It was in the same spirit and impulse to do both that, before we left London, I decided to throw you a birthday party.

~

On the day of your party you wore a red dress, the beads dangling off the fringe, a sash draped across your thin body. The cake cooled on the counter. We popped champagne, chasing our ghosts, cartoons from the late 1950s following the scent of apple pie through an open window, sunflowers turning our corollas with the arc of the sun. Following each other, your twitch to my shiver, my shadow twin, the same as me but different.

You thought I said something condescending and threw a glass of champagne in my face.

We flung emotions off like filmic residue.

Everyone left and we were alone holding each other on the floor.

~

In Potter's film, all of the characters become progressively more histrionic, taking turns playing the role of romantic victim and perpetrator. By the end of the evening, each deceived, betrayed and broken in the process.

I felt the accumulation of hysteria in the film bloom in me with uncanny recognition — the familiar sense of an infinite accretion with nothing to halt it in its path. The spectacle of addiction is just another iteration of emotional despair.

~

The female protagonist in the film is our anti-heroine. Her ascent to political success, her ability to 'act like a woman and think like a man', is cause for celebration. As the party begins, she fields congratulatory phone calls in the kitchen. The kitchen — the space where she tries to perform the domestic obligations of her gender by preparing the food. Thirty minutes later, we see thick smoke billowing out of the kitchen windows, the food blackened and burnt, and her guests rushing in to salvage the culinary disaster.

~

I've been trying to learn how to cook. Since X left, I check on the mouse traps around the cabin and find solace in chopping vegetables. In my process of recovery, I have been trying to take care of myself. I'm reading feminist texts and taking long baths with different scented oils — cedar, basil, rosemary. My recovery from addiction has required a recovery of thought. Maybe it is through these texts that I've also started to feel rage at the binaries of good and bad, trying to wrap my head around the stigma we now carry. Why did we both start to use, first independently, and then together? What moved us from recreational drug use to dependency? Maybe it was just that we really wanted to party.

~

On your birthday I read Lucretius out loud to you.

If things were made of nothing, they would need Noe proper seeds, all things would all things breed. The sea would men produce, from earth would rise Birds, and the scaly race; flocks, from the skies,[...] If generative bodies were not in each kind, How could a certeine mother be to things assigned?[4]

You pretended not to listen while you fussed with the decorations, but I could see it start to percolate as you busied your hands arranging the paper banner above the door. Matter birthing other matter with no regard for genetics was psychedelic, you said — or was it the type of music playing in the background. The shape of our inherited forms harkens back to a presocratic rhythm, my feet and shoulders make way, make wing. The cat sits on top of the spiral. You pour a glass of white wine and the star candies in the fading light.

~

When asked about feminism in an interview in BOMB Sally Potter said:

I have come to the conclusion that I can't use that term in my work. [...] it has become a trigger word that stops people's thinking. [...] There is some way in which the jargon of the radical liberal arena, has become an alienated disservice to its own causes. I also think that the word feminism doesn't imply enough in terms of solidarity with other liberation struggles.[5]

The interview was published in 1993, the year you were born, when intersectionality was a concept just being conceived. Kimberle Crenshaw would first use the term in relation to feminism in 1989, the year that I was born, in a paper she wrote for the University of Chicago. It makes me think that if the female struggle involves the black struggle, the indigenous struggle, and struggles of other oppressed populations, does it also involve the struggle of the addict? Can we take a feminist lens to the stigmas of addiction? Ours was a struggle of white middle-class women, part of the national 'opioid crisis', but what about all the other addicts who don't have the means to seek help and whose struggle results in endless cycles of incarceration? Who is fighting for them?

~

Yesterday I called to see if you felt better. I left you a message, which I'm sure you haven't listened to, about this piece I'm writing in which you and I are the same. I write to you in 'we'. Our bodies are pliant, we shift into each other, a morphing, a metabolic project where I eat and you vomit.

You've spent the last six months puking up everything you eat. The doctors are calling it rumination syndrome. I think about an obfuscation of identity as a type of counter-narrative. I am in the place where our boundaries dissolve and it's hard to remember which is what you have said or — I stub my toe and crack a toenail.

On FaceTime I watch you pull it off, ripping the nail from the corner where it is still attached to the thick of your toe, and show it to me, the translucent sliver with one jagged ripped edge, still partially covered with the flake of some neon green paint, before you lean out of the screen to throw it away.

You love the idea, you say we are already the same. It reminds you of a Lindsay Lohan movie. "So, if I get one of my organs harvested *you'll* wake up without one!"

~

In Potter's film, the characters move between four rooms of a house: the living room, the kitchen, the garden and the bathroom. Through the lens of the camera, the private space is exposed and made public. The viewer becomes a voyeur and witnesses intimate scenes of various emotional breakdowns.

I've never understood how you decide which things you think should be kept private and those you like to make public.

Things you think should be kept private:

bowel movements
feelings
reproductive organs
big words and anything overly intellectual
periods, tampons and anything related to menstruation

Those you like to make public:

makeup
gore
taxidermy
hybrid twinned animals
anal sex
dressing in drag
botox, facelifts and body alterations

Our addiction slots into your list of privacy. You roll your eyes whenever I mention what we went through, you squirm and change the topic. Maybe you aren't yet ready to make it public. We haven't come to terms. But sometimes I wish you would open up, at least to me, and come closer to acknowledging what remains unsaid between us.

~

Most of *The Party* takes place in the living room. In this way it is reminiscent of the drawing room plays developed in Victorian England and put on to entertain guests in the parlour. Also called "drawing room comedies" or "comedies of manners", the plays incorporated dramatic monologues, comedy and, during the transition from the Victorian period to the Modern era, they adapted some form of social criticism.

The social critique of Sally Potter's parlour play constellates around love, politics and middle-class self-involvement. Potter herself has described the film as a portrait of a broken England — the political situation mirrored in the breaking down of each character — the uncovering of truth, the exposing of lies and deception. As I watched the film unfold and the relationships strain under pressure, give in or become fortified in other ways — I had found a mirror for our own harrowing experience.

~

February 4th, 2018 6:59pm Subject: Hello the fuck

Hi Sister Emma,

This is Andrea Rose you may know me as Andy, Patandy or another form, I was wondering if you could FUCKING CALL ME!

Hope your well.
I hear you're not.
This concerns me.

Many thanks,
Andrea your fucking sister

~

An hour after receiving your email, you call on the phone and tell me you aren't feeling well. You're still losing weight, everything you eat or drink immediately comes back up. Your rumination syndrome is defined as 'a chronic motility disorder caused by involuntary muscle contractions and characterised by effortless regurgitation immediately following most meals' — I can't remember where I read that.

At the Mayo Clinic the doctor made you swallow a radioactive liquid to scan your intestines. On our way home five men with guns surrounded you as we waited in line to board the plane. I watched you show them the medical papers to get cleared. Such an American experience, you laughed, and then asked one of the officers if he wanted to frisk you.

I suffer from a different type of rumination. An overwhelming anxiety fixated on the same thoughts and indecisions, running them in a loop and savouring their impact. The anxiety builds in my body and triggers muscle spasms, fatigue, and chronic pain. Maybe there is a cognate relation between the two ruminations, maybe they are counterparts.

You say that when one doesn't feel well they should always wear more makeup. When I ask why, you respond: 'I think of makeup as a kind of protective barrier, it keeps all the bad shit from coming in'.

We lean our phones against the wall and you give me a makeup tutorial over Facetime. The screen is the wall we tapped on when our bedrooms were adjacent, and I have caught your pain, so in response we adorn our bodies.

~

While writing this I remembered that short film I made shortly after we left Recupera called *The Dinner Party*. I dug out the hard drive to watch it. You play a glamorous woman who cuts out the tongue of a man she has tied up at the dinner table. You place his tongue on a cutting board and chop it into chunks you then plop into your soup. There is a close up of you licking blood from your fingers and smiling. The tortured man was played by X.

~

When you turn, I circle. We aren't twins, like our mother Ariadne, but if only her thread could lead us out of our labyrinth, her name an omen, our childhood home an optical illusion, a series of corridors that seem to extend infinitely while each resulting in a dead end. The room distorts, it feels impossible to leave, each new conversation sucking us further in, each blissful distraction adding a bend curving into another passage. I hole up in my room to write but churn out poems like sticks of butter, greasy and rectangular. The room distorts; I crawl out. I make everyone in the house take a stab at writing a poem to mine for material. Yours is the only one I keep. I still have it — my scribbled little talisman — your sloppy handwriting on a piece of pink paper:

Chickens Never Change: a poem by Andrea Rose

Once a chicken never any change
Change won't buy you a chicken
Only that good hard cash.
Cash for chickens is the norm today.
Catching chickens was the norm back then
But now they come in plastic and defeathered.
When I grow up I hope not to be a chicken.
I hope I will need my head to run around
and I hope I still have smooth toes,
not those scaly chicken feet.

~

In Recupera I became so familiar with the sound of your footsteps approaching — dragging and slapping against the floor as they paced the perimeter of the room. I could recognise the sound anywhere.

In one of my journals I even made a mention of it:

March 27th, 2016

Today is Easter Sunday, and so we attempt to resurrect. I watch you pace the room, drag slap drag slap, while they feed morphine through my catheter. I've spent numb hours staring out at the vast impossible horizon through the window. They say each day gets better. We aren't allowed to leave the house; we can't go into each other's rooms. So, we take turns standing at the thresholds of our doorways.

~

A threshold. An impossible horizon.

I remember the big windows in Recupera, the light streaming in, almost blinding. The cold tile floors where our emotions would slip around under our feet. The kitchen with the giant fruit bowl, always full, always offering infinite choice. An impossible horizon.

~

I wonder what our friends must have thought of that birthday party. How they must have looked at each other while we took turns hosting and hiding in the bathroom. Some of them knew, some of them joined us, but we kept it a secret from many of them. We thought we were so sneaky but I'm sure that we weren't. I now think of it as our last hurrah. The last celebration that also commemorated the ending of that dark phase. We were celebrating your birth, your life, but also a rebirth, some part of us needed to die so that we could live. That night, we put it out with your candles.

~

Pop Quiz

E: When we brush our teeth in different countries, do our gestures align?

A: My teeth crumble and your gums recede. The moon aligns us.

E: Is our chewing synchronic? A twinned sweep. A mirror. A reflection that doubles as we see each other in ourselves?

A: Our jaws both pop but I barely chew and you always think there are fish bones stuck in your throat. Funhouse mirrors perhaps.

E: What index would we make if we could archive all the things we have bitten into?

A: Some of them might be Men, food, stuck ropes and zippers, plastic bags filled with food, ice, fingernails. Other things that are stuck.

Notes from Recupera

March 10ᵗʰ, 2016

In Recupera time is not reliable. It is a measure of disorientation. I feel young and old at the same time. I feel a sense of childlike wonder.

As children, we were encouraged to believe in an art that sparked the imagination into reimagining; to favour an expansive sense of reality that encompassed the colourful, the playful, the oneiric. Steeped in this languaging, we interpreted the world around us. Our anarcho-political inheritance was yoked to a sense of play. We learned the history of our resistance movements through our games.

[Act II / Scene i / location: Barcelona]

Our father and his brothers initiate us into the Gran Ducado (The Great Dukedom) — a game developed as children that they continued to play into their adult lives. It started with an argument, someone entered a room and borrowed something without permission, so they tied up pieces of string to keep each other out. The strings became borders, designating the limits of their countries: Lichestein, Ruffino, Tres Triangulos, and Juncara. As the game developed, there were fascist cops, trials, wars, and the terrorist group of La Zao. They stamped papers to borrow items so that every interaction was officially documented and chose action figures to represent dictators or political leaders of each country.

The game is passed down to us. We are given passports and become citizens. Three of our cousins join the terrorist group. My sister and I become journalists from Ruffino sent as undercover spies to their father's country of Lichestein. We learn the harshness of oppression through play. We internalise the terror of fascism through humour. This was before we knew what personal turmoil would come with the loss of innocence, before we understood the intimacy of despair.

~

We were raised in the wake of an oppressive reign, in a country still wounded from decades of living under Francoist dictatorship. For the thirty-six years of Franco's dictatorship, the Catalan language and culture were systematically persecuted. Intellectuals with Catalan ideologies were punished in various ways — tens of thousands were held in concentration camps, some were able to flee and live in exile, while others faced execution. The fascist regime enforced a Catholic worldview which deemed contraception, homosexuality, and behaviour unbecoming of women objects of censorship, but included among these, censors were hired to report and impede any use of the Catalan language. People with Catalan names had to use the Spanish equivalent. It was banned to speak Catalan in schools or in any public space.

Our father doesn't feel comfortable reading or writing in Catalan, his native tongue, but instead reads in Spanish. Sometimes I wonder whether this is a subconscious act of maintaining his identity in the post-war climate, a badge that announces to the world: 'I won't forget how my language was censored and repressed'; or if it is rather some kind of fear that was beaten into him.

little scarab, guess who hit you?

~

III.

Poison

Because she arrives, vibrant, over and again, we are at the beginning of a new history, or rather a process of becoming in which several histories intersect with one another.
—*Hélenè Cixous*[6]

I am reading a book by Silvia Federici and come across an Italian illustration ca. 1385 of a woman walking out of an overgrown garden balancing a tray of spinach on her head. Sister, the wind blows through the leaves in visceral bloom; the black and white of the image pulses, it breathes, the caption on medicinal medieval gardens reads: *A l'edat mitjana, era normal que les dones tinguessin un hort, on cultivaven plantes medicinals. El coneixement de les propietats de les herbes és un dels secrets que transmetien les dones d'una generació a l'altra.*[7] I am reading in Catalan, something wakes up inside of me, yawns, stretches like dust in a sunbeam. I reread the sentence, this time translating it as I go: I*n the middle ages, it was normal for women to have a garden in which to cultivate medicinal plants. The knowledge of the properties of the herbs is one of the secrets women transmitted from one generation to the next.*

We have always been told our maternal grandmother was an herbalist. Versions of the story of her death have been passed around, reassembled, and hidden away, reclaimed in variants. No one agrees; the details are vague. We know that her name was Susan, and that she died in the hills of New Mexico after misidentifying and ingesting poisonous hemlock. I wonder how you would be had you met her; how your figure would contour in rhythm with hers. The poisoning of a body can take on different designs. Hemlock; Heroin; Alcohol; Abuse. Some acting rapidly upon the body, others a slower insidious destruction wearing it down gradually over time.

Popular culture has promoted the idea of poison being a woman's weapon. The common trope of a woman slipping rat poison into her husband's coffee comes to mind. But despite the misogynistic implications of assuming poisoning to be a more subtle and feminine form of killing, cowardly and sneaky, poison is a gender-neutral weapon. In mediaeval times, poison was used as a murder weapon in every social class. Nobility would use poison to dispose of unwanted political or economic rivals. The tradition of clinking our cups together in celebration comes from a fear of being poisoned. Nobles at the dinner table would exchange the liquid in their cups, each pouring a bit of their drink into the others, to prove that they hadn't poisoned the drink of their dinner guest.

While poisoning was done by both men and women, it was the women who were in charge of cultivating the herbs, of maintaining a medicinal cabinet in case someone in the house fell ill. Botanical secrets passed down from woman to woman allowed them to know which herbs to combine to treat various maladies. They were mixed like potions for different purposes: to heal a sickness or to be used as a means of contraception.

Federici explains in her book that the mixing of herbs was sometimes used *to quicken a woman's period, provoke an abortion, or create a condition of sterility.* I remember you taking me to my appointment. At the clinic you placed your hand tenderly on my back as they handed me the photograph in an envelope that I would never open. We cultivate intimacy with small gestures, emotional fulcrums that open us up to each other. Sometimes I wonder if I would have made a different decision had we not been so strung out.

~

Hemlock belongs to the carrot family. It is thought to have first been brought over from Europe to the US and introduced as a decorative plant sometime in the 1800s. It can be fatally mistaken for edible wild parsley, and when accidentally consumed, even small portions of the lethal plant results in respiratory paralysis, coma, and death if treatment is not administered within 3 hours of ingestion. I think of Susan's body slowly shutting down, limb by limb, organ by organ, as she slept in the cabin nestled in the hills. I imagine her death to have been peaceful, like a more-natural-seeming overdose from toxins grown in the woods.

When I ask our grandpa about her death, he tells me that she died, not in the hills as I had always imagined, but in the sterility of a hospital after having her stomach pumped for an hour. When I press further and ask for a death certificate or toxicology report he says, 'it's awkward to be having this conversation and I don't want to talk about it'. He also ingested the hemlock but survived and woke up in the hospital hours later. Perhaps some trauma resurfaced in that conversation that he still carries with him. The lingering traces of a story so harrowing, the unexpected loss of his wife, the mother of his children. Or maybe it's just a frustration with the way memory fails; his inability to retain an accurate account.

Our grandpa was sent to a psychiatric institution at the age of 14 to have 'the femininity zapped out of him' — or so he wrote in a letter he sent to his mother Jane while residing in what he called the 'bobby hatch'. As far as I have pieced together, he was an inpatient for a year and an outpatient for a few years after. When I ask about the electroshock therapy, he says it happened to a friend of his. I know that he loved Susan. He pulls out a photo album and flips through the pages. Among the photos, there are so many handsome young men: 'oh, he's no longer with us'. The AIDS epidemic wiped out most of his lovers and friends. When we get to the photos of their wedding, he says that Susan should have worn her hair down, that he regretted telling her to wear it up.

~

In the few photos I have seen of Susan she looks so young; she wouldn't even live to be 26, the age that you are now, Sister. There is one photo in particular where she is sitting in a field, facing the twins, Ariadne and her brother. It's uncanny how she looks exactly like our mother. Maybe in this way, she lived on through our mother, through her jokes, or the way she builds a fire. The unknown inheritance passed down to then haunt our own gestures. I have imagined Susan, in the high desert air, walking through chamisa and sagebrush, a fine red dust covering her shoes, pointing to various plants and trying to identify the ones she knows, pinching a stem, pressing the herbs between her fingers and savouring their scents, noticing them fade throughout the day. Because she died so young the most vivid memories of her that I have are ones that I have fabricated, the traces of her presence only found in a few photographs and fragments of stories. In each rendition of her death, different people were there: in one our great-grandparents, Bonnie and Johnny, were in the cabin with the twins; in another, Johnny went on the hike (which is sometimes not a hike but a picnic) with Grandpa and Susan when they ate hemlock, and in yet another, Grandpa's brother David was there and also ate the hemlock. In a story so porous, the gaps allow room for the imagination.

I imagine the cabin from things people have told me: gas, wood floors of nailed planks, a little porch, a swing from a tree that oscillates out over a cliff, the Second World War Jeep parked in the driveway that our great-grandpa Johnny drove. Johnny built the cabin in that particular spot because at the bottom of the cliff there is a wild river that runs through the dark canyon where you can find the native New Mexican Rio Grande Cutthroat trout. You can also find hemlock by the water. In one version, the same trail that leads to Johnny's fly-fishing spot is the one that Susan followed down the canyon, rocky and steep, and by the river she identified what she thought to be wild parsley, osha, or watercress (accounts vary).

~

In the Zuni Pueblo of western New Mexico, a type of garden design was developed that is still widely used in many agricultural communities. Waffle gardens are laid out as columns of squares. A grid of raised soil, with a lower bed inside, allows rainfall to reach the plants' roots. The beds of the garden, shaped in squares and placed side by side, together form a grid.

As a structure, a grid is inherently multiple, it repeats itself, the same figure compulsively recurs. The grid offers order, constraint, reiteration, which in turn allows room for freedom and variation. In 'The Originality of the Avant-Garde' the art critic Rosalind Krauss writes: 'The absolute stasis of the grid, its lack of hierarchy, of center, of inflection, emphasizes not only its anti-referential character, but — more importantly — its hostility to narrative'.[8] The grid is not a totalizing system, but rather a poetics of the iterative, a queering of linear narrative. There is no singular narrative but inflections and hues that shimmer in variation. In the story of Susan's death, with all of its versions and inversions, there are so many characters and temperaments feeding into the genealogy, like foils of each other, like squares of a grid, hostile to a singular telling, irreconcilable, they can't come together to form an individual myth.

Great-grandpa Johnny built the cabin where she died. He was a general in the Second World War whose duty it was to clean up the beaches after D-Day. Feet dragging along a deserted beach past craters left behind by bomb explosions in the sand, body parts sticking out half-buried, pieces of artillery left in the ground, burned objects: a backpack, a pair of boots, a helmet, boxes of ammunition unexploded. Foraging for remnants like Susan foraged for edible plants, with death lingering nearby.

They were relegated to cleaning up the beaches of usable ammunition parts after D-Day. The battalion moves, with General Johnny leading them ahead, sifting through the sand, loading the boats that line the horizon with anything they can salvage. Trucks driving the wreckage away towards the docks.

~

Searching through a drawer I find a polaroid of you, Sister, crouching in the garden of the house we grew up in. Your friend looks at the camera while your body leans towards the dirt. Is this one of our inherited gestures?

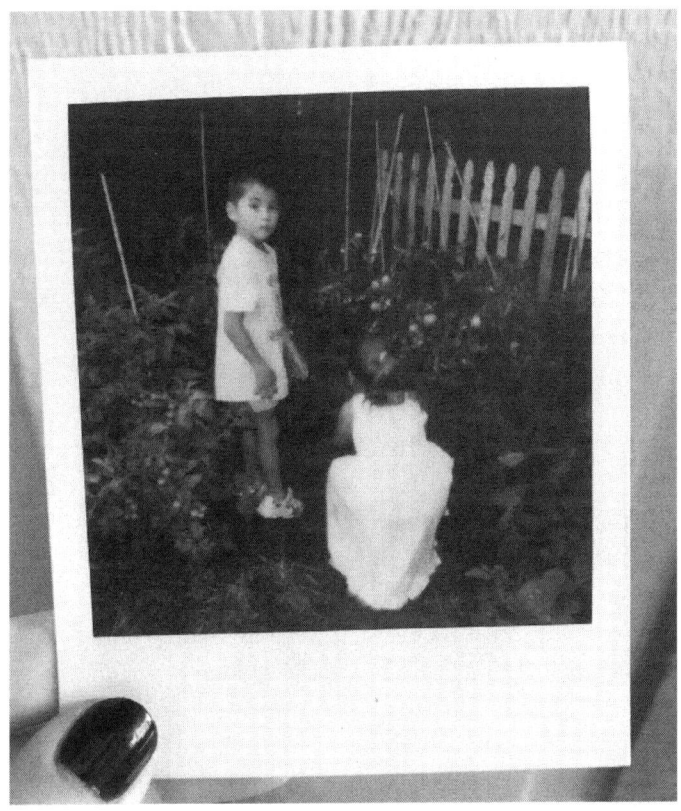

~

Our mother and I drove down to Santa Fe last week. I took notes and watched the landscape pass in the window. We stopped at the Harwood Museum and I spent an hour sitting in the Agnes Martin room while Ariadne wandered in and out. Seven paintings of blue and white, one on each of the walls of an octagonal room, the final section serving as an entrance — an open perimeter. After a trip to Greece, Martin produced a series of ten paintings but designed the room and chose to exhibit only seven. Above the centre of the room is a skylight, I sit on a stool placed directly beneath it. As the light filters in and clouds pass overhead the whitewash blue fades and glows, recedes as the light grows brighter. A cloud passes again, the blue deepens, my eyes unfocus. I slip into a different space, my body wobbles, my head spins. The lines seem to expand and contract, pulsing. A grid imposes itself, lines ripple across thicker lines.

A grid is divided into sections, split apart, but its variants can fold upon themselves. In a grid, there is no original square that is then repeated, rather all squares are repetitions of each other. In the grids used in modernist visual art, the grid overlaid onto the canvas, becomes a doubling of the surface, imposes a geometric order which, as Krauss points out, doesn't reveal the surface but rather renders it opaque.

It was Martin's self-medication, her struggle with schizophrenia calmed by horizontal lines. Her illness assuaged by the flat horizon of the New Mexican landscape. I often feel a similar sense of calm there. The desert expansive, the sunsets dripping over the red earth, the layering sensation of clouds upon blue sky upon shrubs upon dirt.

Sitting in the room Martin designed to house her paintings, I felt the same sense of overwhelming calm. The blue washed over me serenely. The soft lines of pencil marks, the colour flooding between them. The rigidity of the grid fluctuating and warping with the light. Different ranges of hues, washed white over blue over white over blue, thickening layered lines. The squares moved towards me expanding, breathing.

~

Uncle David knew Agnes Martin. He told me a story about how once, frustrated with her work, she tossed it all out her window and into the arroyo. She wanted everything she made before discovering the grid to disappear. Later in her life, she would become reclusive, maybe trying to disappear herself. I wonder if the people in her life felt her absence in the same way Susan's disappearance impacted ours.

~

I ask our uncle what he knows about the story and if he'll take me out to the cabin in the woods of Pecos National Wilderness, down the canyon to the place where she ate the hemlock. He tells me he's already written about it, as if the ground has already been covered, the canvas obfuscated in a veneer of opacity, the remnants looted. He describes the trail as overgrown, the area abandoned.

A few weeks later he sends me his poem. I scan the lines for any information, a description or sense of place. The cabin takes on a gloomy veneer. What had previously been, in my mind, a place to retreat and commune with nature, becomes sinister. Even brightness feels like an invasive presence.

In his last lines I feel the weight of Susan's absence. The void, lacunae caused by absence lingers. The same frustration I feel at trying to piece together this story, is perhaps akin to the more profound void I imagine our uncle to feel at never having known his mother.

About a month later our uncle writes again to tell me that Arthur Sze had also written a poem about Susan's death. In Sze's lines I feel the surreal nature, the lack of narrative implicit in the story of her death.

'Mistaking Water Hemlock for Parsley' by Arthur Sze

Mistaking water hemlock for parsley
I die two hours
Later in the hospital;
Or I turn the shish kebab on the hibachi,
And reel, crash
To the floor, die of a ruptured aorta.[9]

~

Dear Sister,

How does one go about designing a garden? Do I find a patch
of land and lay out a spiralling labyrinth of plants, a grid?
Do I build planters and keep them in the kitchen? The work
of an herb garden is a practice in care, so I am not taking
these decisions lightly. Inside or outside is another question.
Would the planters stack upon each other or lay out flat with
a path between? Do you have any ideas or know anything
about garden design, Sister?

Love,
E

~

A design is the outline of a shape, a plan to carry out the construction of an object or system. It can also, as a noun, be the plan to act out some sort of intention. In ancient Greece, hemlock was used to poison condemned prisoners. After being accused of impiety and corrupting the youth of Athens in 399 BC, Socrates was tried and sentenced to die. With designs on ending his life, he took a potent infusion of the hemlock plant.

I write again, this time to myself:

Does an antidote exist for all of our poisons? Does each poison inevitably lead to death? Were all poisons at some point also used as medicine, as cure? Does all medicine have the potential to poison? Is writing my poison or cure?

~

When Susan died, both her family and his blamed our grandpa for her death. Maybe because, as a man, he was expected to protect his wife, maybe because he was simply just with her. I keep digging, I pore over the photographs, the letters, nothing surfaces but more ambiguity.

~

In Plato's *Phaedrus*, Socrates addresses the ambiguity implicit in the term *pharmakon*. Toxicology is a subfield of pharmacology, a branch of medicine concerned with the uses, effects and interactions of substances, but there is another term found in philosophy and critical theory called the *pharmakon*, which is made up of three parts: poison, remedy, scapegoat. The first two terms come from the Greek word *phármakon* meaning drug. The last comes from the Greek pharmakos which in Ancient Greek religion was the ritualistic sacrifice or exile of a human scapegoat. In this story we have one of each: the hemlock as poison, our grandmother as sacrifice, and grandpa as exiled scapegoat.

~

A text message conversation between our mother, Ariadne, and I, Oct. 11th, 2018:

What do you know about Joan Mitchell?
The singer or the painter?
The painter.
I don't know much but I know her work, she's an expressionist.
Do you like her work?
Yea , although sometimes she's a bit random.
What do you mean?
Just look at her work!
I have, but what do you mean by random?
Just a bunch of strokes.
She has a painting called Hemlock. I really like it.
Why are you looking?
Never mind.

A few days later I tell her what I'm writing about. She tells me I should talk to Pukka, Freddy Pig's girlfriend. When I ask who Freddy Pig and Pukka are, she tells me a strange story about how a Hopi woman cursed Freddy Pig with a medicine pouch and it led to his death.

Later I ask our dad about it and he responds: oh yea, that's true.

~

Plato described the death of Socrates in the *Phaedo:* 'He touched him and said that when it reached his heart, he would be gone'.[10] I think about how the poisoning of a body can take on different designs. My mind moves in patterns that repeat, ruminate, replaying with underlying variation. I picture the same moments, the same images, combining the different stories, piecing things together. My mind wabbles like it did at the Harwood Museum, my eyes blurred, the narrative hiccups, it doesn't come together. The grid shifts out of focus, the squares repeat in iterations, the originality of each story confronted and invalidated by the next.

~

The variety of Hemlock native to Europe is *Conium maculatum*, conium coming from the Greek word *konas* meaning, 'to spin' or 'to whirl,' likely from the vertigo caused when the plant is consumed. I feel myself whirling from one person to the next, one version to the following.

Every attempt to unravel a spool, unknot a thread, has led nowhere. I can't find out anything about Susan. In botany, twinning is the act of that which twines, the act of climbing spirally. I feel myself moving, no longer over the organised squares of a grid, but spiralling, spinning, twisting. I went to visit Susan's grave last weekend and wandered in circles until I found her resting place and wondered who it was that designed her headstone — the flat marker upon which her name is engraved in capital letters except for the seconds, which is in lowercase. There is no last name, no date, just a flat slab that reads SUsAN. There is also a hole in the slab, and I can't tell if it's intentional or not, maybe some sort of modernist artsy flare. I ask our mother and she says there are rumours that there was once a raw diamond encased in glass where the hole is now.

~

A few nights ago, I had a dream in which time was a plane that existed in multiple extensions and truth was a variable in flux. We moved backwards and forwards simultaneously. We were young and old and cooked dinner with our ancestors. I saw you playing with our cousins in the farmhouse, Susan strolled through the fields. My voice moved in a grid, crossing lines and muddling syllables at the places where they intersected, while I narrated your movements.

~

Our grandpa sends me magazine clippings in the mail. One year, with no note attached, he sent me a single peacock feather in an envelope for my birthday. A former curator of the Folk Art Museum in Santa Fe, he now keeps a warehouse filled with antiquities he rearranges in the middle of the night. Amassing a collection worthy of its own museum.

I remember meeting one of his boyfriends when I was young, but most of my life I remember grandpa as being celibate. Agnes Martin was also gay and is said to have struggled with her sexuality. Born a few years before our grandpa, I wonder what struggles she faced. Both lived through or in the wake of the Lavender Scare. As a moral panic spread across the US, President Eisenhower signed an executive order demanding all gay and lesbian government employees be fired from their jobs. I wonder how they experienced it. My grandpa's memories come out hesitantly, he grasps at fragments, fills in the rest.

~

In Plato's *Phaedrus*, the Egyptian god of writing offers writing as a remedy or pharmakon to aid with memory. In Derrida's reading, he determines that Socrates can counteract *pharmakon* with *pharmakon*, because of the ambivalence of the pharmakon of writing which bears its own opposite within itself (as both poison and cure).[11] Do we take poison thinking it can cure us of our ailments? Are poison and cure interchangeable? Is writing a remedy that helps memory? Is writing a kind of poison?

~

Pop Quiz

E: How can bodies translate or make impressions onto other bodies?

A: They translate through wrinkles and rashes, teeth grinding worries. My foot and ugly toe have translated onto me from Papa. You got his eyes, eyelashes that grow inside your eye. My makeup tutorials are translations too.

E: Are we negative and positive impressions of each other, Sister?

A: Yes, we are opposite and the same, bad and good. We influence each other. I might be negative and you bring out the positive. Or we are both negative and that feels more positive sometimes.

E: In the uncanny doubling of our gestures, in the matching tattoos we have of the sphinx lady with a snake tail, are we creating reproductions of each other, Sister?

A: We are just in this life together, pain hand in hand. Ride or die homie.

Notes from Recupera

March 13th, 2016

Having been raised in two cultures means that we are always split. Always home and also homesick, we think in double, a twinned tongue. As I write, I go back to the scenes of our play as a technique of remembering, a line to be traced, followed up the stairs to the room with the bunkbeds where we stayed up with our cousins' telling stories about the witches, *les bruixes*, that lived among the mountains; flashlights beaming under our chins, shadowing their features. The next day we walk in the woods searching the cracks in rocks for the witches' faces. You follow the curve of a nose with your finger, point at the billowing hair made of moss.

~

Our great-great-great grandfather Cels had also been interested in witches. He had passed by the time we were born but shaped our family lore and shifted the family politics by breaking away from the royalist conservatism of his parents and moving towards anarchism. He was an ethnographer, engineer, and poet; a polymath who played an important role in the recording of Catalan oral folklore. I picture him writing in his notebooks as he crossed the country working recording anecdotes, superstitions, common sayings, and songs; his fieldwork resulting in many volumes: *The Catalan Witch*, stories collated from all over Catalunya between 1864-1915 and *The Myth of Popular Tradition* are two of my favourites. On the cover of one of his books, *Zoologia Popular Catalana* published in 1882, there is a scarab placed like a talisman. The *escarabat* of our childhood is an amulet — a seal of protection. I open the book, past the scarab, and find an entry on the *Escarabat bum bum* with the instructions Cels recorded on how to play the game:

<u>*Joch de Criatures, Escarabat bum bum 1801*</u>

Lo qui s'amaga s'agenolla a terra posant lo cap a la falda del qui seu y aquest li ha de tapar los ulls amb les mans de modo que aquell no hi vegi gota. Los demés se posan drets al entorn y, fent voltar Horizontalent los brassos del pit van dhient:

> Escarabat, bum, bum,
> pósahi oli, pósahi oli,
> escarabat, bum, bum,
> pósahi oli, a n'el llum[12]

He wrote the books before the official Catalan dictionary was published in 1931 to regulate grammar. The old phonetic Catalan in his description trips me up while I read. I think of the beetles, their shiny black backs, slowly inching along the patio in the blistering sun. I read the passage again.

~

March 14th, 2016

Cels recorded movements of stories across territories. Language and sayings altering depending on the town or region. He was also involved in establishing public libraries. We grew up in the residue of his thinking; studying in libraries previously filled with water.

[ACT III / scene i / Barcelona, Universitat Pompeu Fabra]

We walk down the long corridors of the library and I picture them rushing with water — covering our ankles and then rising, forming a dreamy wash of floating books. Looking up, in the large reading room that was formerly a water tower, the labyrinth of arches 14 metres high offers the type of serenity proper to a basilica or a cistern and we lower our voices to hushes. In the stacks, we search for and pass around editions of books like sacred objects, opening the covers and analysing the colophons as if they contain some kind of secret code. The emblems — little imprints we photocopy and trade like stamps.

~

With codes and games, we were raised to question the authority of the Spanish state, to believe instead in the subversive magic of books and art. We didn't live in the Spanish empire; instead, we resided in imaginary countries, produced fake passports so we could travel between them. Play was our form of resistance, a way of evading or bringing lightness to the horrors of the world. When a leader, king, or dictator from one of the countries died, we performed a burial and kept the action figures in blocks of ice in Avia's freezer.

I wonder what happened to the graveyard of dictators when Avia moved out of her apartment after Avi died. Maybe the blocks of ice were left to melt like glaciers, slowly revealing protruding body parts.

~

IV.

BLOOD & ICE

growing-growing, the emerald was blood. The stones in the water were eyes and I was not recognized by either the givings or the killings that will make a woman a mother, that will make a mother a moon dropped to the water and carving out her own eye.
—*Sarah Vap*[13]

In my dream we are in Iceland again. There's a black rock floating in the air, a harbinger of winter's dispossession, the sky darkens. A pagan temple is being built for the first time in 1,000 years. At its centre, a gate. We cross a threshold, an act of contrition. You hold a piece of ice to your chest and it melts back through your eye. Your eye falls through the ice. Your nails, shards of blazing orange, mounds of azure behind you.

We are in Iceland and you are asleep in the back seat. We cross frozen ground moving at a swift glide. We undress and dip our bodies into pools of water that, under the moon, glaze our limbs with a metallic shine. In the matted grass under the ice, we imagine fairies, ruby-crowned queenlets. We curve our bodies to toss stones over the surface of the frozen water. The aurora borealis sisters dance above us chasing the blue fox over the hills.

~

Dear Sister —,

Since meeting X everything has changed. He embodies a glacial type of movement. Time carries at strange speeds, like it did in Iceland. Piles of books and papers shift with him as he thinks. Pieces break off and float through conversation. Our ideas congeal in form. Something splits, a calf dislodges, surfaces, sinks back down, slowly glides out of reach, becomes suspended, quiescent, collides into another piece, a draft of wind, a piece of paper drifts to the floor.

Last Sunday we spent the night in a brown motel room where the line thawed between romance and circumstance; between the Murphy bed and maroon carpet. The beige curtains draped heavily onto the floor, like cascades descending upon a sort of groundlessness. The wind rattled the windows through the night. The glow of dawn, a furtive bloom. He pretended to sleep while I wrote: *I'm overwhelmed and fear this might take me over.*

I miss you,
Emma

~

This was before the pregnancy test came back positive. Before the glacier melted and slid into my house. Before his temper burst violently.

Meanwhile you are in London waiting up for G. You wait up every night. He tells you he's on his way. You go to sleep around 4am realising he isn't. He comes home on day five, a sour smell radiating from his pores, his eyes vacant pits, he's been rolling in the dirt. He sleeps, wakes up, goes out again. You try to control your sadness, the anger a green aura smoking off your shoulders.

~

In the motel room
I feel a shiver run through me as X stirs on the bed.

On the drive down, *growing-growing*, an emerald increase, a becoming; on the way back a blue burning had left my body with a surge of bloodlets. Pieces dislodged, flowed through me. Everything is a process: cloud, miscarriage.

I wanted to call you, but something was frozen inside of me. To move at a glacial pace you must take on a slowness, claim it as your own, drag yourself heavily, fling a crystal film across the surface. To experience something frozen you must shut down, you must shut yourself down, you must become numb.

~

When you look through a piece of ice, objects take on a shapely dysmorphia, the opacity of the frozen water blurs the image. The contours of a hand fall away, it becomes an amorphous swell blending into the sidewalk. Through the ice, everything becomes indistinct, nothing is in focus, vision deceives, nothing is precise. Just a swell of emotion.

You fly home and I pick you up from the airport. Lines of mascara streaming down your cheeks.

We cross over frozen ground moving at a swift slowness.
Everything blurred like your face behind the glass. A pagan
temple is being built. At its centre, a gate.
We cross a threshold.
XOXO

~

Pop Quiz

E: What is the future of the prosthetic limb, of the body?

A: It's art. Personalised beauty. It's robotic and empowering. It's unique. The possibilities are endless.

E: Did the addition of an ear-shaped cartilage to the body of the mouse, represent the possible dangers of body alteration as well as potential progress in the medical field?

A: No no no. It's beautiful. It represents hope, how amazing science can be to help missing-eared people feel themselves again. It's like a kidney transplant. It's sci-fi.

E: How are good and bad contained within the same capacious metaphor?

A: Like laughing at someone falling cuz it ain't you? Like vomiting to get clean? Like it sucks but it's only gonna get better? Rock bottom is the only way up.

E: As bodies are altered, does their original shape soften? Do we obscure by adding and become vague?

A: No no no. The scar tissue hardens. It heals tougher. The trauma and scars capture memories in time.

Notes from Recupera

March 16th, 2016

Recupera is a place that is no place. It is suspended from reality. We don't have phones here, or access to our computers. But we have books, pens, and notebooks.

[ACT IV / scene i / Barcelona / night]

After several meetings with the Russian philosopher and encounters with the anarchist ideology, Cels helped disseminate Bakuninism throughout Catalunya. Our anarchism played out in subtle inflections. At a table of 30 Avia throws the dinner plates on the floor — tired of washing so many dishes, she laughs while she shatters the ceramics in an act of refusal.

[ACT IV / scene ii / Barcelona Zoo]

We meet our cousins by the back entrance of the zoo. Leaning against the brick wall, we listen to the elephants wailing, the birds keening. We are carried by the sounds to a wild place where animals run free and make charming noises. *The Barcelona Zoo contains the only albino gorilla in the world, his name is Copet de Neu.* I whisper to you as if divulging a secret, one which initiates you into the realm of the older children. We cup the wall with our hands to speak to Snowflake the gorilla, devising a plot for his liberation, imagining that once freed he will come play with us, a thinking imbued with the type of magic a child invokes to procure an imaginary friend.

~

March 17th, 2016

Around the time I turned six I became obsessed with Egypt. Africa is just on the other side of the Mediterranean, and I'm afraid the lions will come up and eat us. The hexagonal tiles of the bathroom floor converge into lion's faces and follow me everywhere. I put my finger on the globe and show you how close it is, trying to convince you into accompanying my fears.

On the bookshelves here in Recupera, I found a book that says that for the Egyptians, the scarab symbolises resilience and rebirth. In Ancient Egypt it was believed the balls of dung rolled by the scarab contained the eggs from which the next generation would hatch. When we did hatch, we picked up our lineage, took it with us, carried it as our own. The scarab is our emblem, colophon, our poesis or making, a remaking, a generative little bug with its stick-like legs crawling along carefully as if through a viscous atmosphere it is resisting, rolling a ball of shit across the ground, lifting the sun up out of darkness. We were raised in refusal, taught to move one leg slowly and keenly before placing it down again, to press firmly through viscosity, to learn all the accents, singing as we walked with our cousins in the woods.

~

Revolt against the State is a much easier undertaking, because there is in the very nature of the State something that is an incitement to revolt.

—Mikhail Bakunin[14]

~

March 18th, 2016

A poet once told me about little poems we can carry like shivs in our pockets, to take out and use whenever we need. The lines serving as a shield or protection; the repetition, a sort of mantra or anthem, building strength.

Escarabat bum bum posa-hi oli posa-hi oli.

~

March 19th, 2016

[ACT V / Ibiza / summer]

Running on cobblestone, you fall and split your lip, you still bear the trace, the line of a faint scar. Can there be resilience without the spilling of blood? What shivs do we need to arm ourselves? You press a napkin to your mouth and, in an attempt to distract you, I lead you to the shade of a tree and read you tales that come from across the Strait of Gibraltar. Scheherazade arms us with shivs. *the next day she resumed her narrative.*[15]

~

March 20ᵗʰ, 2016

The shiv repeats the phrase, a knife that repeats the act of slicing through. We split apart from our families but carry inherited shapes as we forge ahead. The thing world, materialist and formed of atoms bears witness to our imagination, it moves and transforms with our imaginings, becomes something idiosyncratic, original. We mould our shapes — they are not fixed but handed down to us. The names we give our origins, and the mythologies of our upbringings, bind us to our historiography.

[ACT VI / the Black Mountain / dawn]

Scarab backwards phonetically reads as barracks, so we assemble. Climbing down from our bunkbeds, we cross the field, past the water basin, and up a small path spangled in succulents where we find the deserted quarters once meant for the *masovers* who tended the land, the stewards of the farm; the lodgings become our barracks.

~

March 21st, 2016

With the start of Franco's dictatorship, the 18th century palace that housed the Parliament of Catalunya in Barcelona, was seized, and used as temporary military barracks. The hub of Catalan political dialogue was commandeered to house a sinister, oppressive violence. Until 2004 it wasn't returned fully to the reinstated Parliament of Catalunya. Just up the street, there are shrapnel scars on the church walls, and what was once the headquarters of an anarcho-syndicalist group, the CNT, is now an Apple Store. The gates into the city are guarded by a KFC and a McDonalds. Even architecture is malleable, the city effaced and turned into a Disneyland ruin. We now live under an insidious cruelty, the reign of capitalism.

Forty-five minutes outside of the city in the Montnegre the clouds roll in, we witness the morphing of their shape, a temporal quality of transience; something grows, decomposes, an oscillation. We were raised to believe in water fairies and surrealist performance, subscribed to the seductive dream, but the trace we carried with us was just a dream. We were not taught how to be financially responsible, how to take care of ourselves in a world void of imaginary economies. So, when the silk cocoon split open and a new modernity emerged, we took out our shivs and flung off our old forms; moulds, casts, shapes left uninhabited; silhouettes, imprints, things that formed our nuanced disavowal. Clothes left behind that no longer fit us. We assumed our identities:

I am a sculptor.
I am a journalist from La Zau.
I am a writer.

I am a Catalan.
I am a woman.
Etc.

~

March 21st, 2016

[ACT VIII / the Black Mountain / night of Sant Joan]

Once a year we sit around the flames of a fire that burns all night and share our sacred stories, the peculiar mythologies that craft the forms of our family lore. On midsummer's eve, the night of Sant Joan, *the nit de foc or night of fire*, we spell our names weaving sparklers through the air, watching the traces linger.

Around the embers and in this light the stories of Cels are passed down. We learn his arm was run over by a cart, that it gangrened and had to be amputated. I remember you cross-legged listening to our uncle.

Cels is the plural of sky in Catalan; the clouds part and we spread the blanket open. We lay down on the patio to watch the stars cross and fall through the sky, watching their traces linger.

~

The only photo I have ever seen of Cels is the one that populates his Wikipedia page. In the photo he sits with legs on either side of a backwards facing chair, his arms crossed over the top, obscuring the upper bannister. His gaze set directly on the camera, his eyes are kind, inquisitive, playful, the black beret tilted to the side and wrinkles lining his face, provide the true aura of a European intellectual of the early 1900s. His left hand seems to be holding a folded-up piece of paper, or a handkerchief, that obscures one of the lateral bannisters. It is impossible to tell if the object is a note to a friend, a scrap of paper where he scribbled down an anecdote overheard, or an old cloth rag to blow his nose.

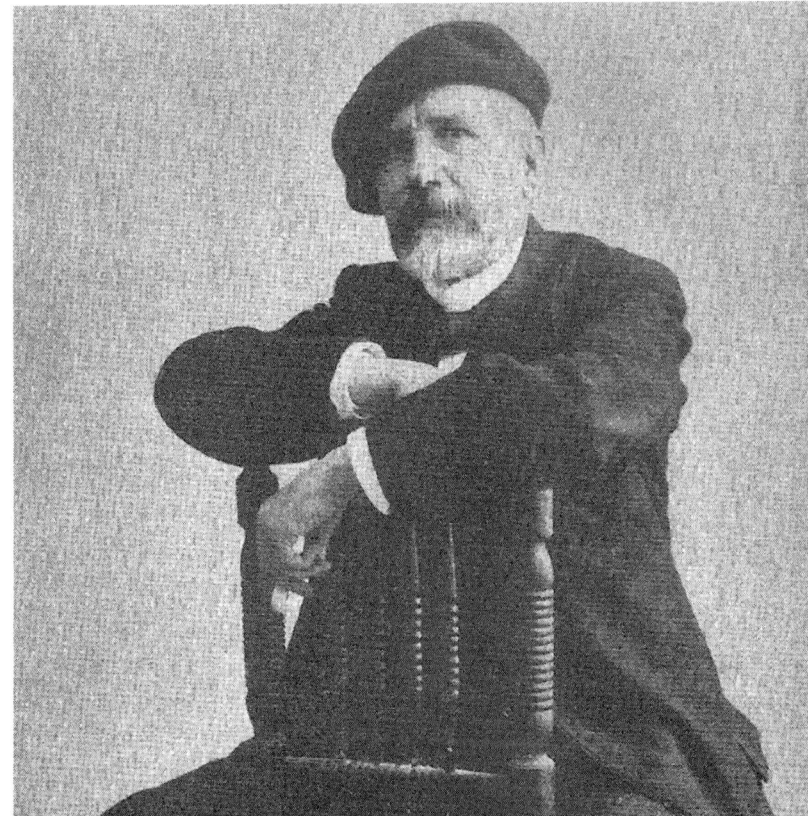

In the early Fourth Dynasty, there first appeared in the hands of statues what the American Egyptologist Henry Fischer, former curator and head of Egyptology at the Metropolitan Museum of Art in New York, refers to as an 'elusive shape'. In their fisted hands, many of the figures sculpted during this period seem to be holding a mysterious oval object. Along with other art historians, Fischer argues that 'the only object in the repertory of Old Kingdom iconography that corresponds to the more usual form of the "elusive shape," both in contour and color, is a bolt of cloth'.[16] He goes on to point out that the hieroglyph that represents a handkerchief is also similar to that of the bolt of cloth and that both could be potential solutions for the mystery of the elusive shape. Fischer writes that 'if cloth has, by its very nature, an elusive shape, assuming, among other shapes, the one that is found in the hands of Egyptian statues, it also lends itself to a variety of uses. Thus it is not surprising to find a piece of cloth occasionally in the hands of women, children, or prisoners, who would not ordinarily be expected to hold a staff or baton'.

The piece of cloth becomes an object accessible to all, regardless of class or gender; it could be found in the photographed hand of Cels, the hands of Catalan *puntaires*, or of an Egyptian king. Cloth is a neutral material, used in making garments, upholstery, bed linen; it is also used to obscure things from view, to cover the hands of the magician as he performs a trick. It was the fabric found in our hands as we flung a sheet over a string we had tied between two trees; in this way, we suspended the backdrop for our plays, useful in case we needed someone to stand behind it with a hose spraying upwards in a scene where it was raining.

~

March 24th, 2016

[ACT IX / the Black Mountain]

As a child, a sheet is infinitely mutable, easily becoming a
ghost, a backdrop, a parachute. Sometimes we would use the
sheet to make an elephant, with one person bent forward,
hinging from the hips, and placing their hands on the waist
of another in front of them, we would hang the cloth over
their two bodies. The person in front would stick out one arm
and sway from side to side to act as the trunk. Then, a third
person, the elephant trainer, would lead the elephant onto the
stage, and ask for a volunteer from the audience. The volunteer
would be asked to lie prone on the floor, and the elephant
would slowly and hesitantly step over the volunteer's lower
back, but as soon as the first person had stepped over, the
second, who played the role of the elephant's rear, would pour
a glass of water onto the volunteer lying unsuspecting on the
floor. The trainer, dismayed, would help the wet volunteer up,
apologising profusely for his elephant having peed on them.

~

March 24th, 2016

Draped in cloth that made elusive shapes, we traded colophons and tapped escarabat bum bum. In our barracks on the black mountain, we wrote a manifesto. The censors found it. Now this is all that remains.

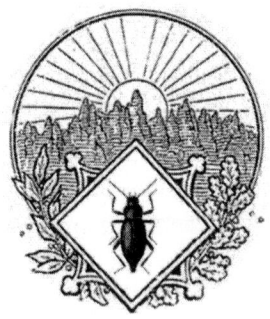

~

Memory is a Ghost

I can't remember if you were speaking to me or not as we boarded the plane; or during the nine-hour flight from London to Recupera where we passed out and woke up shivering. I can't remember who picked us up and drove us across the border.

You were angry because I had called our parents. When I did, you said you would never speak to me again. But I called because I saw what was happening to you — the darkness, your shaking. You were disappearing. I called for you. When our dad picked up the phone, I could only let out a few small words, you need to come here. He arrived the next day. At first, I couldn't tell him what was happening, a swell in my throat occluded my language. When I finally broke past the blockade, I told him about you. It was too much to acknowledge my own sickness. You would have to tell him about me. A week later Ariadne came. They started planning how to get us to Recupera.

We were lucky to have their support. Our parents stayed after we left for Recupera to help some of our friends get out too. But there are so many who don't get out, I keep thinking.

~

So many are put on synthetic substitutes that are equally as harmful to what they're trying to wean off. The pharmaceutical industry has too much at stake. There is nothing human in capitalism. When we arrived at Recupera, I kept thinking of a line from Dianne di Prima: 'I have just realized that the stakes are myself'.[17]

After days of morphine injections, we ate from a plant and fell into a dark dream that buzzed incessantly for twenty-four hours. In mine, there was an evil grinning monkey pulling shards out of my body. I wonder what you saw in yours.

~

I'll leave the last Pop Quiz for you here, you can take your time, there is no due date:

> What can we do in order to recover?
> What rituals?
> What gestures of care?
> What antidotes?
> Can we recover through play?
> What does recovery look like?
> When, if ever, does it end?

~

Epilogue

My sister has given me permission to share everything and anything. She has insisted on not altering any of what I write and has supported me through writing this text every step of the way.

My sister embraces the confessional mode in her own art practice. She now dedicates her time to making grotesque, beautiful, and strange erotic sculptures. You can follow her on Instagram @deadratlove69. Here is what she said when I asked her what she thought about the confessional as an artistic mode:

> I've always liked the idea of a confessional box. In a way it is a lot like a glory hole, it takes place in the same-shaped cubical boxes you get in and you're looking for a release from a faceless stranger. Putting your dick through a hole and speaking private truths without knowing who's there to take it in both take a lot of vulnerability. But a box has many different meanings and like surreal language can represent a hole inside you. Make your own language. Imagine you could stick your head straight up your own ass, scream your regrets and no one could hear you. I'd do that a lot. Two great things would happen if that were possible. You would experience an internal vibration of ecstasy and pain, but it would be total self-gratification because your own screams would be responsible, it would be a double release. Not just for the internal vibrations but for the internal space of judgment free enclosure to confess. Your ass box makes you cum

with your own sufferings because of its release from painful memories. Don't get fingered by a priest do it yourself! This is the time to create that judgment-free enclosure. Internally confess through artistic design, creating your own language.

~

ACKNOWLEDGEMENTS

A large portion of this manuscript was written at the Jack Kerouac School of Disembodied Poetics at Naropa University from 2017-2019. I am grateful to my friends and mentors in Colorado who supported me in writing this. Anne Waldman, Jeffrey Pethybridge, J'Lyn Chapman, and Julie Carr.

Thank you to everyone who has read and offered feedback. Lisa Robertson, Sophie Seita, Hannes Gauch, Nina Ellis, Corinne Dekkers, Nathan Wheeler, Natalie Earnhart, Benoit Loiseau, Kole Fulmine, Salome Kiner, Azad Sharma, Yvonne Westbrook, Eva Schestag, and my parents.

Thank you to my sister who has come to every reading I have ever done and has always supported my writing.

A version of 'Poison' was published under the title 'KArEN' in *The Denver Quarterly issue 52*, 'My Catalogue of Casts' was published by *The BitterSweet Review issue 1*.

Thank you to the Jan Michalski Foundation. My residency in the cabins provided me with the conditions to finish this manuscript.

Endnotes

[1] Oliver, Akilah, via HR Hegnauer, question posed in a poetry workshop during the 2007 Summer Writing Program at Naropa University www.are.na/block/22028544.

[2] Bellmer, Hans, quoted in Hal Foster, *Compulsive Beauty* (MIT Press, 1993), p.109.

[3] Iijima, Brenda. *Eco language reader* (Nightboat Books, 2010).

[4] Lucretius, excerpt from *On the Nature of Things* in *Revolution: A Reader*, edited by Lisa Robertson and Matthew Stadler (Paraguay Press, 2012).

[5] Firlot, Shari, Sally Potter quoted in 'Interview with Sally Potter' *Bomb Magazine* (July 1, 1993), https://bombmagazine.org/articles/1993/07/01/sally-potter/.

[6] Cixous, Hélene, 'The Laugh of the Medusa', *Signs* Vol.1 No.4 (University of Chicago Press, 1976) pp. 875-893 https://www.jstor.org/stable/3173239

[7] Fedirici, Silvia, traduît per Marta Pera Cucurell, *Caliban i la bruixa: Dones, cos I acumulació primitiva* (Virus Editorial, 2018).

[8] Krauss, Rosalind E. *The Originality of the Avant-garde and Other Modernist Myths.* (MIT Press, 1986).

[9] Sze, Arthur. "Mistaking Water Hemlock for Parsley". *The Redshifting Web: New & Selected Poems.* (Copper Canyon Press, 1998).

[10] Plato. *Plato's Phaedo.* (Oxford: Claredon press, 1911).

[11] Derrida, Jacques, 'Plato's Pharmacy', *Dissemination*, trans. Barbara Johnson (London: The Athlone Press, 1981), pp.61-172.

[12] Gomis, Cels, *Zoologia Popular Catalana* (Tip. L'Avenç, Barcelona, 1910).

[13] Sarah Vap, *Viability* (Penguin Books, 2016), p.12.

[14] Bakunin, Mikhail, *No Gods, No Masters: An Anthology of Anarchism* ed. by Daniel Guerin (AK Press, 2006), p.152.

[15] *Tales from the Thousand and One Nights*, trans. by NJ Dawood (Penguin Classics, 1973).

[16] Fischer, Henry G., 'An Elusive Shape within the Fisted Hands of Egyptian Statues', *Metropolitan Museum Journal*, v.10 (1975) https://resources.metmuseum.org.

[17] di Prima, Diane, 'Revolutionary Letter #1', *Revolutionary Letters* (City Lights Publishers, 1971).